YOU
choose

No Hitting, Henry

Don't Hurt

Lisa Regan

It might be useful for parents or teachers to read our 'How to use this book' guide on pages 28–29 before looking at Henry's dilemmas. The points for discussion on these pages are helpful to share with your child once you have read the book together.

First published in 2013 by Wayland
Copyright © Wayland 2013

Wayland, an imprint of
Hachette Children's Group
Part of Hodder & Stoughton
Carmelite House
50 Victoria Embankment
London EC4Y 0DZ

Produced for Wayland by Calcium
Design: Emma DeBanks
Editor for Wayland: Victoria Brooker
Illustrations by Lucy Neale

Dewey number: 302.5'4–dc23

ISBN: 978 0 7502 8344 1
15 14

Printed in Dubai

An Hachette UK company
www.hachette.co.uk
www.hachettechildrens.co.uk

Contents

Hello, Henry!

Henry is feeling **cross**.
When he gets angry, he sometimes
hurts other people. He doesn't
mean to hurt, but he just
feels so **upset**.

Follow Henry as he finds himself in tricky situations in which he must learn to stop hitting and choose to stay **calm**.

YOU
choose
too!

Stay calm, Henry

Henry and his big brother Ben are playing hide and seek.

Ben is **cheating** and it's **ruining** Henry's game.

What should Henry choose to do?

7

Should Henry:

a burst into tears and kick the car?

b tell Ben that he won't play any more if he cheats?

8

c fight his brother?

Henry, choose **b**

Sometimes you can make things much better by staying calm. Telling people how you feel can **fix** a problem. Hitting and punching just makes things even worse.

What would **YOU** choose to do?

Be brave, Henry

Henry is watching a group
of children having lots of fun.

Henry **feels** the children are leaving him out of their game.

What should Henry choose to do?

Should Henry:

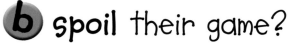 kick one of
the children?

b **spoil** their game?

c ask the children if he can join in?

Henry, choose **c**

Bad feelings can make you want to kick and punch, to show other people that you're hurting inside. This also makes other people feel bad! Try to be nice and that will make you feel happier, too.

What would YOU choose to do?

Ask for help, Henry

Amit has taken the toy train that Henry was playing with.

That's not **fair**!
It's spoiled Henry's game.

What should Henry choose to do?

Should Henry:

a tell a grown-up?

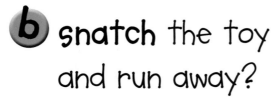

b snatch the toy and run away?

c **pinch** Amit to make him give the toy back to Henry?

Henry, choose **a**

Pinching will hurt others and get you into trouble. Count to 10 quietly to give you time to calm down. Then tell a grown-up what has happened.

What would **YOU** choose to do?

Be helpful, Henry

Dad wants Henry to walk nicely round the shops instead of running off.

But it's so **boring** at the shops!

What should Henry choose to do?

Should Henry:

a) **whack** Dad and cause a scene?

b) sit on the floor and **refuse** to move?

c hold Dad's hand and ask if he can help to choose the food they buy?

Henry, choose **c**

Doing grown-up things can be boring. But if you smack and kick it just makes things worse for everyone. Imagine how you would feel if someone smacked or hit you!

What would **YOU** choose to do?

Talk about it, Henry

Janeka has pushed in front of Henry in the lunch **queue**.

That's not allowed! Henry feels **angry** with Janeka.

What should Henry choose to do?

Should Henry:

a tell Janeka that she needs to join the end of the queue?

b jab his tray into her back until she moves again?

c push her out of the queue?

Henry, choose **a**

It's okay to feel cross when somebody else is not fair. Learn to explain how you feel. That way you won't get into trouble for hitting and hurting others.

What would **YOU** choose to do?

Well done, Henry!

Hey, look at Henry! Now he can make all the right choices, he's feeling much **happier**.

Did you choose the right thing to do? If you did, big cheers for you!

If you chose some of the other answers, try to think about Henry's choices so you can stop yourself from hitting and hurting next time. Then it will be big smiles all round!

And remember – don't hit, it hurts!

How to use this book

This book can be used by a grown-up and a child together. It is based on common situations that pose a challenge to all children. Invite your child to talk about each of the choices. Ask questions such as 'Why do you think Henry should talk to his brother Ben instead of hitting him?'.

Discuss the wrong choices, as well as the right ones, with your child. Describe what is happening in the following pictures and talk about what the wrong and right choices might be.

• Most people feel cross if something goes wrong. Everyone has to learn how to feel angry without hurting others.

• If other people do the wrong thing, hitting won't help. You will end up in trouble even though they did something wrong first.

● Hurting people or spoiling their fun can make people not want to play with you next time.

● There are many ways to hurt someone. Hitting, kicking, spitting, pinching, smacking and name-calling all hurt.

Explain that lots of things happen that can make people feel cross. It's okay to feel angry, but it isn't okay to take it out on other people. Ask your child to think about what happens when they lose their temper. Do they get into trouble or upset their playmates?

Try to think of ways your child can make the anger go away. Teach them to stop and take a deep breath, or count to 10, and then think about how they want to behave. Show them how good it feels to stay in control!

Glossary

calm not angry or cross

cause a scene to behave in a bad way
  that makes other people notice you

cheating ignoring the rules of a game

fix to solve a problem in order to make
  it go away

pinch to nip or squeeze someone's skin

queue to line up while waiting for something

refuse to not do something when asked

ruining spoiling something or breaking it

snatch to grab or take something
  in a rude way, without asking for it

spoil to destroy something

whack to hit

Index

Titles in the series

Like all children, Annie sometimes gets really, really angry! She has lots of choices to make – but which are the CALM ones?

ISBN: 978 0 7502 8349 6

Like all children, Carlos sometimes does things that are wrong, and doesn't come clean. He has lots of choices to make – but which are the TRUTHFUL ones?

ISBN: 978 0 7502 6724 3

Like all children, Charlie sometimes feels a little scared. He has lots of choices to make – but which are the BRAVE ones?

ISBN: 978 0 7502 6722 9

Like all children, Gertie sometimes plays a little dirty. We put Gertie on the spot with some tricky problems and ask her to decide what is FAIR!

ISBN: 978 0 7502 6725 0

Like all children, Harry sometimes takes things that don't belong to him. He has lots of choices to make – but which are the HONEST ones?

ISBN: 978 0 7502 6723 6

Like all children, Henry sometimes gets angry and sometimes he hits, too. He has lots of choices to make – but which are the GENTLE ones?

ISBN: 978 0 7502 8344 1

Like all children, Sam sometimes feels sad, and he doesn't know how to make himself feel better. He has lots of choices to make – but which are the HAPPY ones?

ISBN: 978 0 7502 8350 2

Like all children, Tilly wants to do everything *right now*, and sometimes she just can't wait! She has lots of choices to make – but which are the PATIENT ones?

ISBN: 978 0 7502 8343 4